Cricket Never Does

A Collection of Haiku and Tanka

Other Books by Myra Cohn Livingston

ORIGINAL POETRY

Flights of Fancy and Other Poems
4-Way Stop and Other Poems
Higgledy-Piggledy: Verses and Pictures
I Never Told and Other Poems
Monkey Puzzle and Other Poems
Remembering and Other Poems
There Was a Place and Other Poems
Worlds I Know and Other Poems
Cricket Never Does

(*Margaret K. McElderry Books*)

ANTHOLOGIES

A Time to Talk: Poems of Friendship
Call Down the Moon: Poems of Music
Dilly Dilly Piccalilli: Poems for the Very Young
If the Owl Calls Again: A Collection of Owl Poems
I Like You, If You Like Me: Poems of Friendship
Lots of Limericks
Poems of Christmas
Riddle-Me Rhymes
Roll Along: Poems on Wheels
Why Am I Grown So Cold? Poems of the Unknowable

(*Margaret K. McElderry Books*)

PICTURE BOOK

B Is for Baby: An Alphabet of Verses
with photographs by Steel Stillman

(*Margaret K. McElderry Books*)

Cricket Never Does

A Collection of
Haiku and Tanka

Myra Cohn Livingston
illustrations by Kees de Kiefte

MARGARET K. McELDERRY BOOKS

Some of the verses in this book have appeared before in the following Myra Cohn Livingston titles: *Flights of Fancy and Other Poems, 4-Way Stop and Other Poems, Monkey Puzzle and Other Poems,* and *Remembering and Other Poems.*

Margaret K. McElderry Books
An imprint of Simon & Schuster Children's Publishing Division
1230 Avenue of the Americas
New York, New York 10020

Designed by Ethan Trask/Nina Barnett
The text of this book is set in 15-point Perpetua.
The illustrations were done in pen and ink.

Printed in the United States of America

10 9 8 7 6 5

Library of Congress Cataloging-in-Publication Data

Livingston, Myra Cohn.
Cricket never does : a collection of haiku and tanka / Myra Cohn Livingston ; illustrated by Kees de Kiefte.
p.   cm.
Summary: A collection of more than fifty original haiku and tanka verses about the four seasons.
ISBN 0-689-81123-3
1. Seasons—Juvenile poetry. 2. Children's poetry, American. 3. Haiku, American. 4. Waka, American. [1. Seasons—Poetry. 2. Haiku. 3. Waka. 4. American poetry.]
I. Kiefte, Kees de, ill. II. Title.
PS3562.I945C75   1997
811'.54—dc20
96-30528
CIP
AC

Contents

Spring 1

Summer 11

Autumn 21

Winter 33

Index of First Lines 41

Spring

Whirring from fuchsia
to fuchsia, the hummingbird
shops for his dinner

Long green fingernails
grow and split, holding up white
magnolia blossoms

Balanced on a crane,
the tree surgeon ministers
to a sickly palm

Now and again, clouds
shift, break apart, showing off
a lost world of blue

How the birds quarrel
among themselves this morning
over one small worm!

Shiny colored tents
pop up above people's heads
at the first raindrop

On the tree, a peal
of tiny bells . . . on the ground,
lavendar litter

One long crack in the
pavement—an endless freeway
for commuting ants

Slowly the ocean
sucks in its breath, letting it
out with a gurgle

For one instant, a
green curving wall, and then a
burst of white ruffles

Squawk at the ocean,
seagulls, it will still roar out
much louder than you

How angry you are
today, Ocean, as your waves
knock me off my feet!

No matter how hard
wild waves push, brown kelp beds stay
anchored in ocean

Whatever you have
to say, Mockingbird, tell it
to me in a hurry—
the blue jay wants some equal
time to complain about you!

Bougainvillea spills
over stone walls, trying to
hide the graffiti

Along railroad tracks,
junkyards lie camouflaged in
pink oleander

Look how the birds turn
the telephone lines into
a musical staff!

On Easter Sunday
our maples still wear their old
tattered brown dresses

Summer

Not wishing to stop
his chirping the whole night long,
Cricket never does

Here go the willows
again, dragging their long sleeves
into the river . . .

Who has the better

right to smell the first summer

rose, bee—you or I?

Wild branches, spilling
over the concrete wall, reach
out to touch the bus . . .

Leaning against each
other comfortably, birch
watch down the highway . . .

Hemlocks build themselves
their own dark houses, their own
tall secret castles . . .

Pines, tamed by fences,
pop their heads over to look
out at traffic . . .

One willow escapes
to sun herself on the soft
grasses of summer . . .

Even in summer,
bees have to work in their orange-
and-black striped sweaters

Only a blue jay
would swoop down so low trying
to annoy our cat!

What mermaid found this
yellow scallop shell, waved it
like an open fan . . .
dressed herself in bright white coral
and bewitched a green merman?

Surfers, cresting the
tops of the tallest waves, rise
up and disappear . . .

Skyscrapers drown in
Central Park's lake like a fleet
of sunken galleons . . .

Even the moon lies
on its back, rolling over
to stare into space

Sprawling across the
sides of a dry aqueduct—
naked graffiti

How could I sleep through
August nights without the sharp
music of crickets?

Stalking my garden
each night, quietly feasting
in a dark corner . . .
What appetite hungers for
nothing but sweet basil leaves?

Autumn

In silver armor,
the lizard, felled by rain, dreams
of his summer sun

One by one, circling
down to earth, these yellow birds,
these frail, falling leaves

The first day of school . . .
does my teacher wonder who
these new faces are?

Quiet morning fog . . .
suddenly pierced by the voice
of an angry crow

One last patch of sky
about to be swallowed up
by thundering clouds . . .

What a strange carpet
the rain weaves with its pattern
of leaves and brown twigs . . .

Another raindrop
and the stream will overflow
into the meadow . . .

Searching for only
one clear puddle, I find my
rain-drenched reflection . . .

When the rain has stopped,
Mourning Dove, you can begin
your singing again . . .

One chrysanthemum
in a vase, watching over
Second Avenue

Floating in by way
of last night's late weather news . . .
a piece of lost storm

There goes Sun, again,
just beginning to slide down
the eucalyptus

Peeking from her room,
parting thin white cloud-curtains,
Lady Moon smiles

Ocean, how do you
know when to curve and make of
the earth a round ball?

Eclipsing the sun,
Moon leaves, for a moment, a
golden wedding ring . . .

Looking into a
dark midnight river, Moon sees
no one but herself

Outside the walls of
townhouse gardens, weeds grow in
happy abandon

We pass old friends still
living in California—
the eucalyptus

Old rags hold fast to
bare bushes near the freeway,
waving me along . . .

Close your eyes! Feel the
pale eyeballs of a dead cat . . .
two peeled purple grapes

Winter

The moon rides so low
tonight I mistake it for
a wayward canoe

These are not foaming
white horses, but only waves
in a wild ocean

Wet newspapers cling
to a chain-link fence, settling
themselves for winter

Suddenly earth, sky,
tree, and mountain are carried
off, shrouded in fog

Seagulls also stand
marveling as ocean waves curl
and crest, curl and crest

Changing before my
eyes, purple clouds hovering
above the ocean
rise high, higher, into a
range of towering mountains

Here we are, Winter,
just you and I in the snow,
freezing together

In between downpours,
Crow ventures out to survey
the damage below

Piles of ragged leaves,
flung together, huddle up
against winter's chill

Now that Christmas is
over, poinsettias are
busy dropping leaves

Snow sits on cold steps
leading to the front door, and
waits for my return

Now that December
has gone, the sun stays on the
hilltop much longer . . .
waiting for me to climb up
and watch as it disappears . . .

Index of First Lines

Along railroad tracks,...9
Another raindrop...25

Balanced on a crane...4
Bougainvillea spills...8

Changing before my...37
Close your eyes! Feel the...32

Eclipsing the sun,...29
Even in summer,...16
Even the moon lies...18

Floating in by way...26
For one instant, a...7

Hemlocks build themselves...15
Here go the willows...13
Here we are, Winter,...38
How angry you are...7
How could I sleep through...19
How the birds quarrel...5

In between downpours,...38
In silver armor,...23

Leaning against each...3
Long green fingernails...9
Look how the birds turn...29
Looking into a...29

No matter how hard...7
Not wishing to stop...13
Now and again, clouds...4
Now that Christmas is...39
Now that December...40

Ocean, how do you...28
Old rags hold fast to...31
On Easter Sunday...10

On the tree, a peal...6
One by one, circling...23
One chrysanthemum...26
One last patch of sky...25
One long crack in the...6
One willow escapes...15
Only a blue jay...
Outside the walls of...30

Peeking from her room,...27
Piles of ragged leaves,...39
Pines, tamed by fences,...15

Quiet morning fog ...24

Seagulls also stand...37
Searching for only...25
Shiny colored tents...5
Skyscrapers drown in...18
Slowly the ocean...7
Snow sits on cold steps...40
Sprawling across the...19
Squawk at the ocean,...7
Stalking my garden...20
Suddenly earth, sky,...36
Surfers, cresting the...17

The first day of school...24
The moon rides so low...35
There goes Sun, again,...27
These are not foaming...35

We pass old friends still...30
Wet newspapers cling...35
What a strange carpet...25
What mermaid found this...17
Whatever you have...8
When the rain has stopped,...25
Whirring from fuchsia...3
Who has the better...14
Wild branches, spilling...15